Once Upon a Time

Three Favorite Tales

Retold by **Jim Aylesworth**
Illustrated by **Barbara McClintock**

SCHOLASTIC INC.
New York Toronto London Auckland Sydney
Mexico City New Delhi Hong Kong Buenos Aires

The Gingerbread Man   ISBN 0-590-97219-7

Text copyright © 1998 by Jim Aylesworth.

Illustrations copyright © 1998 by Barbara McClintock.

Book design by David Saylor

The text was set in 14-point Edwardian Medium. The display type was hand lettered by Chris Costello.

The artwork was rendered in watercolor, sepia ink, and gouache.

The Tale of Tricky Fox   ISBN 0-439-09543-3

Text copyright © 2001 by Jim Aylesworth.

Illustrations copyright © 2001 by Barbara McClintock.

Book design by David Saylor

The text type was set in 16-point Colwell Roman. The display type was hand lettered by David Coulson.

The artwork was rendered in watercolor, black ink, and gouache.

Goldilocks and the Three Bears   ISBN 0-439-39545-3

Text copyright © 2003 by Jim Aylesworth.

Art copyright © 2003 by Barbara McClintock.

Book design by David Saylor

The text was set in 14-point Edwardian Medium. The display type was hand lettered by Kevin Pyle.

The artwork was rendered in watercolor, sepia ink, and gouache.

All rights reserved. Published by Scholastic Inc. SCHOLASTIC and associated logos

are trademarks and/or registered trademarks of Scholastic Inc.

12 11 10 9 8 7 6 5 4 3 2 1   4 5 6 7 8 9/0

Printed in Singapore 46

This edition created exclusively for Barnes & Noble, Inc.

2004 Barnes & Noble Books

ISBN 0-7607-6099-3

First compilation printing, November 2004

Book design by Alison Klapthor and David Saylor

The Gingerbread Man

The Tale of Tricky Fox

Goldilocks and the Three Bears

Notes About the Stories

THE GINGERBREAD MAN

"The Gingerbread Man" is an example of a cumulative tale, with a simple, repetitive plot and lots of rhythm. The most commonly told version of this folktale was first published under the title "The Gingerbread Boy" in the *St. Nicholas Magazine* in May 1875. The story epitomized a new philosophy of children's literature that caught on in the latter part of the nineteenth century that advocated reading for pleasure rather than for instruction. Special thanks to Karen Van Rossem for her help in researching the roots of this story. The *St. Nicholas* version and more source notes can be found in *World Folktales* by Atelia Clarkson and Gilbert B. Cross, Charles Scribner's Sons, 1980.

THE TALE OF TRICKY FOX

For many years readers have loved this traditional trickster tale based on the "trading" motif. An early version from Massachusetts, called "The Travels of a Fox," was first collected by Clifton Johnson, and was originally printed in *The Outlook* in 1897. Johnson was one of the first Americans to gather Anglo-American folklore. This version can be found in its original form in *What They Say in New England and Other American Folklore* (Carl Withers, ed.), Columbia University Press, New York, 1963. Special thanks to Marilyn Iarusso for her help in leading us to earlier versions of this tale.

GOLDILOCKS AND THE THREE BEARS

An early version of this beloved story was entitled "The Story of the Three Bears" and was written down in 1837 by a poet named Robert Southey. Today, he is most remembered with Coleridge and Wordsworth as one of the Lake Poets. Southey's version featured an old woman instead of a little girl. As storytellers told and retold his story, the old woman disappeared in favor of the little girl. Her name, of course, is Goldilocks, and she is one of the best-recognized characters in children's books. Special thanks to Karen Van Rossem for her help in tracing the history of this story. Excellent source notes can be found in *The Classic Fairy Tales* by Iona and Peter Opie, Oxford University Press, 1974.

The Gingerbread Man

Once upon a time,

there was a little old man and a little old woman.

One day, the little old woman said, "Let's make a gingerbread man!"
"Yes, let's do!" said the little old man, and they did.

So, they mixed up the batter,

and they rolled out the dough,

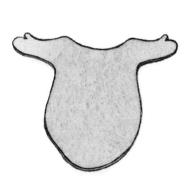

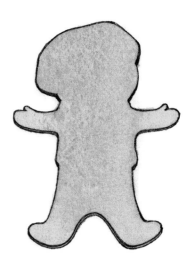

and they shaped
the little arms,

and they shaped
the little legs,

and they shaped
the little head.

And with raisins, they made the little eyes and the little nose and the little mouth, and then with sugar glaze, they dressed him in a fancy suit of clothes.

When all was set, they put the gingerbread man into the oven, and they waited.

Pretty soon, a delicious smell coming from the oven told them that the gingerbread man was ready, and so were they!

But when they opened the oven door, out popped the
Gingerbread Man, and he ran across the floor.

The little old man and the little old woman could hardly believe their eyes! The Gingerbread Man looked up at them, put his little hands on his hips, and said,

"Run! Run!
Fast as you can!
You can't catch me!
I'm the Gingerbread Man!"

The little old man reached down to grab him, but quick as a wink, the Gingerbread Man ran out the door and down the road, and the little old man and the little old woman ran after him.

"**Come back! Come back!**" they yelled. But the Gingerbread Man just looked over his shoulder, and said,

"No! No!
I won't come back!
I'd rather run
Than be your snack!"

And he kept on running.

And he ran,

and he ran,

and he ran,

and after a time, he met a butcher standing in front of his shop. The Gingerbread Man looked up at him, put his little hands on his hips, and said,

"Run! Run!
Fast as you can!
You can't catch me!
I'm the Gingerbread Man!
I've run from a husband!
I've run from a wife!
And I'll run from you, too!
I can! I can!"

The butcher reached down to grab him, but quick as a wink, the Gingerbread Man ran on down the road, and the butcher ran after him!

"**Come back!**" yelled the butcher.

And not far behind, the little old man and the little old woman were yelling, too! "**Come back! Come back!**"

But the Gingerbread Man just looked over his shoulder, and said,

"No! No!
I won't come back!
I'd rather run
Than be your snack!"

And he kept on running! And he ran, and he ran, and he ran.

And after a time he met a black-and-white cow. The Gingerbread
Man looked up at her, put his little hands on his hips, and said,

"Run! Run!
Fast as you can!
You can't catch me!
I'm the Gingerbread Man!
I've run from a husband!
I've run from a wife!
I've run from a butcher
With a carving knife!
And I'll run from you, too!
I can! I can!"

The black-and-white cow reached out to grab him. But quick as a wink, the Gingerbread Man ran on down the road, and the black-and-white cow ran after him!

"Come back!" yelled the black-and-white cow.
And not far behind, the little old man, and the little old woman, and the butcher with the knife were yelling, too!

"Come back! Come back! Come back!"
But the Gingerbread Man just looked over his shoulder, and said,

"No! No!
I won't come back!
I'd rather run
Than be your snack!"

And he kept on running.
And he ran, and he ran, and he ran.

And after a time, he met a muddy old sow.

The Gingerbread Man looked up at her, put his little hands on his hips, and said,

"Run! Run!
Fast as you can!
You can't catch me!
I'm the Gingerbread Man!
I've run from a husband!
I've run from a wife!
I've run from a butcher
With a carving knife!
I've run from a cow
All black and white!
And I'll run from you, too!
I can! I can!"

The muddy old sow reached out to grab him. But quick as a wink, the Gingerbread Man ran on down the road, and the muddy old sow ran after him!

"Come back!" yelled the muddy old sow.

And not far behind, the little old man, and the little old woman, and the butcher with the knife, and the black-and-white cow were yelling, too!

"Come back! Come back! Come back! Come back!"

But the Gingerbread Man just looked over his shoulder, and said,

"No! No!
I won't come back!
I'd rather run
Than be your snack!"

And he kept on running.

And he ran,

and he ran,

and he ran.

And after a time, he met a fox. The Gingerbread Man looked at him, put his little hands on his hips, and said,

"Run! Run!
Fast as you can!
You can't catch me!
I'm the Gingerbread Man!
I've run from a husband!
I've run from a wife!
I've run from a butcher
With a carving knife!
I've run from a cow,
And a muddy old sow,
And I'll run from you, too!
I can! I can!"

"What did you say?" asked the fox. The tricky fox pretended that he couldn't hear well. "I'm not as young as I used to be," he said. "You'll have to come closer and speak louder."

The Gingerbread Man stepped closer, and in a very loud voice, he said,

"Run! Run!
Fast as you can!
You can't catch me!
I'm the Gingerbread Man!
I've run from a husband!
I've run from a wife!
I've run from a butcher
With a carving knife!
I've run from a cow,
And a muddy old sow!
And I'll run from you, too!
I can! I can!"

Just then, the little old man, and the little old woman, and the butcher with the knife, and the black-and-white cow, and the muddy old sow came running around a turn in the road! And they were yelling!

"Come back! Come back! Come back! Come back! Come back!"

The Gingerbread Man looked over his shoulder, but before he could say a single word, the fox jumped up and grabbed him!

And quick as a wink,
Before he could think,
With a snap and a snick,
And a lap and a lick,
The Gingerbread Man
Was gone!

The little old man, and the little old woman, and the butcher with the knife, and the black-and-white cow, and the muddy old sow all stood and stared sadly at the fox. He hadn't left a single crumb for anyone.

Riddle-riddle ran, fiddle-fiddle fan,

So ends the tale of the Gingerbread Man.

The Tale of Tricky Fox

A NEW ENGLAND TRICKSTER TALE

"Once upon a time," began the kindly teacher, "in woods that aren't so very far away..."

. . .Tricky Fox was bragging to Brother Fox. "Stealing chickens is too easy!" said Tricky Fox. "I'm going to get me a fat pig!"

"I'll eat my hat if you do!" said Brother Fox. "There ain't no fox in this whole wide woods that can even carry a fat pig."

"I could!" said Tricky Fox. "If I was to fool a human into putting one into a sack for me, I could! I'll show you!"

And Tricky Fox, he picked up his sack, and he ran off into the woods.

Tricky Fox ran, and he ran, and he kept on running until just before it started getting dark. Then he stopped, and he picked up a little piece of log, and he put it into his sack.

Then he knocked on the door of a nearby cottage.

When a lady opened the door, Tricky Fox hunched over like he was feeble, and in a rickety voice he said:

"I'm on my way to
Bonny Bunny Bay.
The night grows cold,
And I'm so old.
Please let me stay."

The lady felt sorry for him, and she said, "Okay, I'll let you stay, but no tricks!"

"Oh, no!" said Tricky Fox. "I'm so worn out, I can't think of anything but curling up in front of your fire. I'm just worried about my sack, is all. I don't like for anyone to look in it, and I'm too tired to guard it."

"Don't worry," said the lady. "Leave it with me. I won't look in your sack."

"I know you won't," grinned Tricky Fox, and he handed her his sack and pretended to fall asleep.

But before the lady went to bed, she couldn't resist a quick peek into that sack even though she said she wouldn't.

"Just a piece of log," she said to herself.

Then she blew out the light, pulled up her covers, and fell asleep.

Pretty soon, Tricky Fox heard her snoring.

Quiet, quiet, quiet, he went over, *tippy toe, tippy toe,*

pulled out that piece of log, and he put it on the fire.

Then, he went to sleep, sure enough.

In the morning, Tricky Fox held up his empty sack, and he said, "What's happened to my loaf of bread?"

"You didn't have a . . ." the lady began to say, and then she stopped herself, remembering that she wasn't supposed to know what was in that sack.

"I don't rightly know," she said, too embarrassed to admit the truth. "Must have been the mice. I'll give you a loaf of mine." And she opened up her bread box and put a loaf of her bread into Tricky Fox's sack.

"Thank you very kindly," said Tricky Fox, and he took the sack, and he ran off into the woods. And as he ran, he sang this sassy song:

"I'm so clever ~ tee-hee-hee!
Trick, trick, tricky! Yes, siree!
Snap your fingers. Slap your knee.
Human folks ain't smart like me."

All day long, Tricky Fox,
he hung out in the woods until
just before it started getting
dark again.

Then he knocked on the door
of another nearby cottage.

A lady opened the door, and Tricky Fox hunched over, and in a rickety voice he said:

"*I'm on my way to Bonny Bunny Bay. The night grows cold, And I'm so old. Please let me stay.*"

This lady felt sorry for him, too, and she said, "Okay, I'll let you stay, but no tricks!"

"Oh, no!" said Tricky Fox. "I'm just worried about my sack, is all. I don't like for anyone to look in it, and I'm too tired to guard it."

"Don't worry," said the lady. "Just leave it with me. I won't look in it."

But even so, this lady couldn't resist a quick peek into that sack, either. "Just a loaf of bread," she said to herself, and she went to sleep.

When Tricky Fox heard her snoring, quiet, quiet, quiet, he went over, *tippy toe, tippy toe,*

took out his loaf of bread...

... and he gobbled down the whole thing. Then he went to sleep, sure enough.

The next morning, Tricky Fox held up his empty sack, and he said, "What's happened to my chicken?"

"You didn't have a . . ." the lady began, and then she stopped herself, remembering that she wasn't supposed to know what was in that sack.

"I don't rightly know," said the lady, too embarrassed to admit the truth. "It must have flown out the window. I'll give you one of mine." And she took the sack, and she headed out to her henhouse.

When she was gone, Tricky Fox,
he danced around, and he laughed,
and he sang his sassy song:

"*I'm so clever ~ tee~hee~hee!*
Trick, trick, tricky! Yes, siree!
Snap your fingers. Slap your knee.
Human folks ain't smart like me."

And when she came back,
Tricky Fox took the sack, and he
ran off with it.

All day long, Tricky Fox hung out in the woods until just before it started getting dark again. Then he knocked on the door of another nearby cottage.

A lady came to the door, and Tricky Fox hunched over, and in a rickety voice he said:

> "*I'm on my way to*
> *Bonny Bunny Bay.*
> *The night grows cold,*
> *And I'm so old.*
> *Please let me stay.*"

This lady felt sorry for him, too, and she said, "Okay, I'll let you stay, but no tricks!"

"Oh, no!" said Tricky Fox. "I'm just worried about my sack, is all. I don't like for anyone to look in it, and I'm too tired to guard it."

"Don't worry," said the lady. "Just leave it with me. I won't look in it."

But this lady couldn't resist a little peek, either. "Just a chicken," she said to herself, and she went to sleep.

And just as it had happened before, when Tricky Fox heard her snoring, he went over, quiet, quiet, quiet, *tippy toe, tippy toe,*

and he took out that chicken and he let it loose.

In the morning, Tricky Fox held up his sack, and he said, "What's happened to my pig?"

"You didn't have a . . ." the lady began to say, and then she stopped herself, remembering that she wasn't supposed to know what was in that sack.

"I don't rightly know," she said, too embarrassed to admit the truth. "Must have slipped out the door. I'll give you one of mine." And she took Tricky Fox's sack, and she headed out to her pigpen.

When she was gone, Tricky Fox danced around, and he laughed, and he laughed, and he sang his sassy song:

"I'm so clever ~ tee~hee~hee!
Trick, trick, tricky! Yes, siree!
Snap your fingers. Slap your knee.
Human folks ain't smart like me."

But Tricky Fox hadn't counted on one important thing, and that was that this particular lady was a teacher. And Tricky Fox didn't know that teachers are not so easy to fool as regular humans are. And this lady had gotten suspicious, and she'd come around the side of her house, and she'd watched through the window as Tricky Fox danced and laughed and sang that sassy song of his.

"That rascal!" she said to herself. "I'll fix him!" And instead of going over to her pigpen, she went over to her doghouse.

And instead of putting a pig into Tricky Fox's sack, she put in her bulldog.

And then she brought it back, and Tricky Fox hefted it onto his shoulder and ran off.

When Tricky Fox got home, Brother Fox was waiting for him. And when Brother Fox saw that sack, which looked for all the world like there was a fat pig inside of it, he sadly took off his hat, and, true to his word, he began biting and chewing, and biting and chewing until it was gone.

Then Tricky Fox untied the sack.

And to their sorry surprise, out jumped that lady's bulldog! And that bulldog, he bit 'em low and bit 'em high, and he made the fur just fly, fly, fly! And then, he chased 'em off into the woods.

". . . And because of what happened that day," said the teacher; "every fox in the woods has learned a lesson. And because of what happened, every fox in the woods has been much more respectful of humans. And because of what happened, you never hear foxes singing sassy songs. And because of what happened, you never, ever see one wearing a hat."

GOLDILOCKS AND THE THREE BEARS

Once upon a time, there lived a little girl named Goldilocks, who was very, very good, except that sometimes she forgot to do things that her mother told her to do. Yes she did.

Fortunately, most of the things she forgot to do were small things, like forgetting to tie her shoe or forgetting to wipe her mouth after eating bread and jam, and so it didn't matter too, too much.

But once in a while, Goldilocks would forget not to do things that her mother told her not to do, and that kind of forgetting would lead to much more serious trouble. . . .

. . .Very like the trouble that happened on the day of this story.

It all began one sunny morning when Goldilocks asked if she could go out onto the meadow to pick flowers.

"You may go," said her mother. "But make sure not to go into the woods! I've heard that a family of bears lives there."

"Yes, ma'am!" said Goldilocks, and she picked up her flower basket and she left out the door.

But very soon, she saw a butterfly, and she began to chase it. And, as luck would have it, that butterfly led her to the very edge of the woods. And then, just then, Goldilocks saw a pretty yellow bird. And wanting to see more pretty birds, she forgot not to do what her mother told her not to do, and she followed a path up into the woods looking for pretty birds.

Very soon, Goldilocks came to a curious little house there in the woods.

And oh, she thought it was so pretty that straight away she peeked in through the kitchen door.

In the meantime, the family of bears who lived there had just left out the front door for a walk while their bowls of breakfast porridge cooled off on their kitchen table.

"Hello!" called Goldilocks. "Anybody home?"

Well, there was nobody home, of course, and Goldilocks should have turned around and gone back to the meadow.

But oh, it was ever so pretty and curious inside there, that, even though her mother had told her not to go into people's houses without being invited, she forgot not to, and she went in anyway.

Straight away, she saw those porridge bowls on the kitchen table. And *mmm*, yes! That porridge smelled so delicious that I'm afraid she forgot that her mother had told her not to touch other people's food, and she decided that she had to have a taste. And she did.

First, she took a taste from the great, huge papa-bear bowl, but oh my, no! That porridge was much too hot!

So then, she took a taste from the middle-sized mama-bear bowl, but that porridge was too cold.

And so then, she took a taste from the wee, small baby-bear bowl, and she found it neither too hot nor too cold, but just right. And so delicious, that without really meaning to, she ate it all up.

Then, she went into the parlor. And there, she saw three curious chairs. Goldilocks thought they were the most curious chairs that she had ever seen.

In fact, they seemed so curious to her that even though her mother had told her not to use people's things without permission, she forgot not to, and she climbed up, and she sat down in the great, huge papa-bear chair.

But after only a moment or two, she found that this great, huge chair was much too hard for her.

So she climbed down, and she sat in the medium-sized mama-bear chair. But this chair was too soft for her.

So next, she sat in the wee, small baby-bear chair. And this chair she found neither too hard nor too soft, but just right.

But when she leaned back to make herself more comfortable, it broke and dropped her onto the floor with a *CRASH!*

Well, you might think that being dropped on the floor like that would have put a stop to her being so curious, but no, it didn't, sadly no.

For just then, Goldilocks saw the curious little stairs, and she was so intrigued that she went up them.

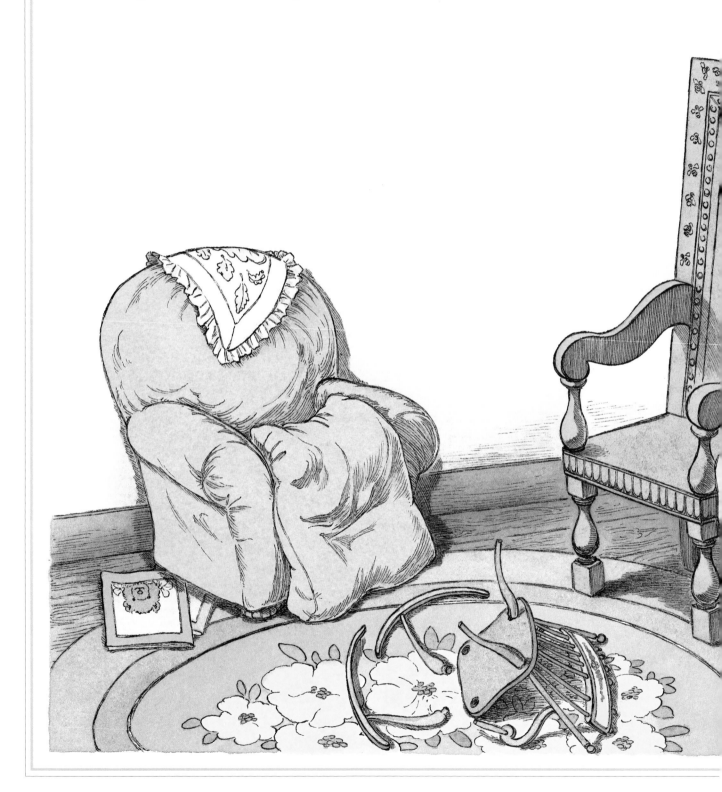

At the top, she found an even more curious and pretty room, and even though her mother had often told her not to be nosy about other people's private business, she forgot not to, and she went in. And there she saw three curious beds.

And straight away, she climbed up into the great, huge papa-bear bed.
But very like the great, huge papa-bear chair, Goldilocks found it too
hard for her.

So she tried the medium-sized mama-bear bed, but like the mama-bear chair, she found it too soft for her.

And so last, she tried the wee, small baby-bear bed. And yes, she found it neither too hard nor too soft, but just right. And so very, very comfortable that without really meaning to, she fell sound asleep.

Then, just then, the bear family returned from their walk.

The great, huge papa bear went over to the kitchen table, and in his great, huge voice, he said,

"Someone's been eating my porridge!"

Then the mama bear looked at her bowl, and in her medium-sized voice, she said,

"Someone's been eating my porridge!"

And then the baby bear looked at his bowl, and in his wee, small voice, he said,

"Someone's been eating my porridge, and they ate it all up!"

Then they went into the parlor.

"Someone's been sitting in my chair!"

said the papa bear in his great, huge voice.

"And someone's been sitting in my chair!"
said the mama bear in her medium-sized voice.

"And someone's been sitting in my chair!"
cried the baby bear in his wee, small voice.
"And they broke it all up!"

Cautiously, the bears went up the stairs.

The papa bear looked at his bed, and in his great, huge voice, he said,

"Someone's been sleeping in my bed!"

"And someone's been sleeping in my bed!"
said the mama bear in her medium-sized voice.

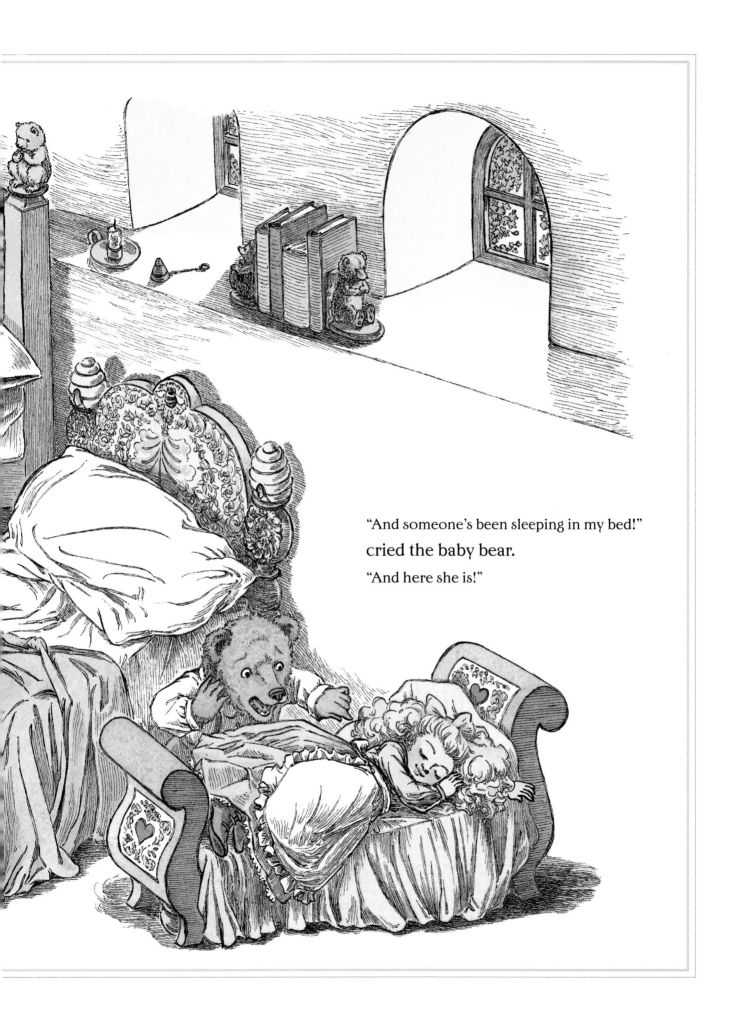

"And someone's been sleeping in my bed!"
cried the baby bear.
"And here she is!"

Then, just then, Goldilocks woke up, and she looked up at the bears who were looking at her! And just as fast, she remembered that her mother had told her not to talk to strangers, and she didn't do it! No, indeed, she didn't!

Instead, she ran down the stairs,

and she ran through the kitchen and she ran out the door...

...and she ran, and she ran, and she ran all the way home.

And from all that I've heard, Goldilocks's scary experience there in the woods that day did wonders to improve her young memory. And while it's true that she still sometimes forgets to do small things like tying her shoe or wiping her mouth after eating bread and jam, Goldilocks never, ever forgot not to do what her mother told her not to do ever, ever, ever again.